FOX &

by Beth Ferry

illustrated by Gergely Dudás

RABBIT

AMULET BOOKS · NEW YORK

CONTENTS

STORY ONE

FAIR, FIREWORKS & FRED

I just made that up.
I didn't really see a crab.
Stop copying me.

I wasn't copying you. I was just being nice.

Humph.

Have you tried the popcorn? And the funnel cake? How about the lemonade? The food here is fantastic.

The rides here are fantastic. Who's up for the Ferris wheel?

It's very high.

It's very fun.

It's super high.

It's super fun.

Are you sure?

Sure as sunshine.

What happens if I get scared?

I will win you a stuffed lion! Then you can squeeze the stuffing out of it if you get scared.

3 TICKETS = 1 PRIZE

Or you could eat a super frozen frenzy cone. That'll give you courage.

That'll give you brain freeze. Come on. Let's try the fishing game.

There's something fishy about this game.

These balloons are unpoppable.

POP!

POP!

Wheeee!! This is super-trooper fun.

Whoa! This is higher than I thought.

You need this more than I do.

Oooh look, fireworks!

What is Fred?

Fireworks + Red = Fred!

Let's name him Fred.

All the best names start with F. Oh . . . and R too.

Come on. Let's go home.

!

Please. Pretty please. Pretty please with a frozen frenzy cone on top! I just want to win once!

WHEEL OF FORTUNE

I won! I won! I'm a winner! I'm a spinner! I'm a spinner winner! I'm a super duper loop-the-looper cotton candy dinner winner. I'm a...

Stop! The whole fair knows you're a winner.

What'd I win?

Plastic? Plastic? I won a lousy piece of plastic? No fair!

SAND, SWIMMING & SUNSET

Hurry up!

What's taking so long?

The sun will be setting soon.

Do you want to pack the toilet too?

Fred is getting antsy.

Ta-da! I'm ready!

You're not bringing anything?

Oh, yeah.

Because flip-flops start with F.

Have you tried the french fries? And the pizza? And the ice cream? The food here is fantastic.

The water here is fantastic. Who wants to go in?

I need to put on sunblock.

The water's super-trooper warm! Come on.

I need to set up the umbrella. And beach towels. And chairs. And . . .

The waves are amazing. Come in.

It's almost lunchtime.
I have to arrange the sandwiches.
And slice the pickles.
And pluck the grapes.
And pour the tea.
And . . .

Wow. That was awesome.
Ready to swim?

Oh, no.
We just ate.
We have to wait now.

Are you afraid to swim?

Me? Afraid? Absolutely not.

Then come on.

It looks like a hole to me.

Oh, well **that** is a hole, but **this**, this is the Mountain of Munch. It chomps anything pinchy or pointy or bite-y or scary.

Well, this can be the Hole of Hunger. It can eat everything that scares us.

I hope it's hungry, because everything in the ocean scares me.

Take that, pinchy lobster!

In you go, scary squid!

Meet your doom, orca whale!

Get lost, tiger shark!

Smell you later, killer crab!

29

SURPRISES, SWAMPS & SEEDS

39

What are you doing?

Didn't you see that?

There's a very high hill. And a very wild wilderness. And a very stinky swamp.

I saw.

There's a very high hill! I hate heights.

I know.

There's a very stinky swamp! You hate swimming.

I know.

But we should go anyway.

What????? Seriously? Are you serious? You can't be serious.

We found a map in a bottle. I mean, how cool is that?

Pretty cool.

Very cool.

41

You're not bringing anything?

Oh, yeah.

Because flashlight starts with F.

Climb the
Very Highest
Hill

It worked!

Of course it did. And I could really use a sandwich.

Hooray! We're almost there!

50

They're just frogs!

Poisonous frogs?

Well, I don't think so. They look like regular old frogs.

There are over 100 types of poisonous frogs.

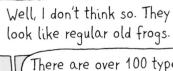

Um, I think those live in the Amazon.

Are you willing to risk your life for a surprise that might not even be a good surprise?

For a zinger?

Ribbit!

It **was** easy!

Wait! Are we on Surprise Island?

Yup!

Where are the surprises?

Maybe we need to walk around a little.

Oh!

What? What surprised you?

Just this ladybug.

Oh.

Oh!

What? What do you see?

Just those dandelion puffs.

Oh.

Maybe the surprise is that there are no surprises because we expected surprises so now we're surprised there are none.

Grrrr!

This stinks. Let's go.

Go back across the stinky swamp and the wild wilderness and the really high hill? No way!

Wait, what's that?

Oh.

What is it?
Money?
Marshmallows?
Macaroni?

Um, no.
Just some seeds.

Seeds?
Oh.
I guess that's surprising.

You mean disappointing.
We came all this way
for nothing!!

Maybe surprises don't have to be big like piñatas or parties or volcanoes.

Yeah. Maybe surprises can just be ladybugs and rainbows.

Yeah. Or a day with your best friend.

Double yeah!

What'd I miss?

GARDENING, GROWING & GROANING

I do!!

I am an expert gardener.
A gardening expert.
I am skilled in the art
of growing the most
delicious things to eat.

Will you teach us?

With pleasure!

First rule:
DIG DEEP.

Huff.

Puff.

Moan.

Sweat.

Whine.

Slump.

I'm tired!

I'm double tired!

Second rule:
DIG DEEPER.

Why is the ground so hard?

Why is the dirt so hard?

Because gardening is hard work! But eating is easy. So keep going!

Third rule:
SOW SLOWLY.

Sow?

It means "plant."

How will we know what these are?

We'll just have to wait and see.

It'll be a surprise!

A seed surprise!!

Surprise Island really did give us a surprise!

Fourth rule:
WATER WISELY.

It was me!
Me!
I'm the
zinger!
I ate
the garden!

Fox?

I couldn't help myself. I just nibbled the lettuce to see how it tasted. Then I decided I should try the tomatoes because they looked sort of green instead of red. And the peas practically fell into my mouth.

And before I knew it . . .

I'm so, so sorry.

Vegetables are hard for you to resist, aren't they?

Double extra super extremely hard.

I think I understand.

I'm super-trooper very berry sorry.

I know. It's OK. I forgive you.

You do?

Yes.

Are you sure?

Sure as salad!

What'd I miss?

SQUEEZE, SWEET & SOUR

They're getting bigger.

And bigger.

And bigger.

And they're turning the color of sunshine.

It's a lemon tree!

A beautiful lemon tree!

Look at all the lemons!

Should we pick them?

Yes!

Are you sure?

Sure as sour.

La la la.

Lo lo lo.

Le le le. Lemonade!! Get your lemonade here!

Lemonade? Lemonade? I love lemonade! And orange juice. And cranberry juice. And slushies.

We only have lemonade.

Made from lemons.

From lemons we grew ourselves.

Yum!

I flew around the playground 50 times so I would be hot and extra thirsty! Can I please have all the lemonade?

We did it! We sold all the lemonade! What will we do with all the money?

Something amazing!

READ ON FOR A SNEAK PEEK OF
FOX AND RABBIT'S NEXT ADVENTURE IN

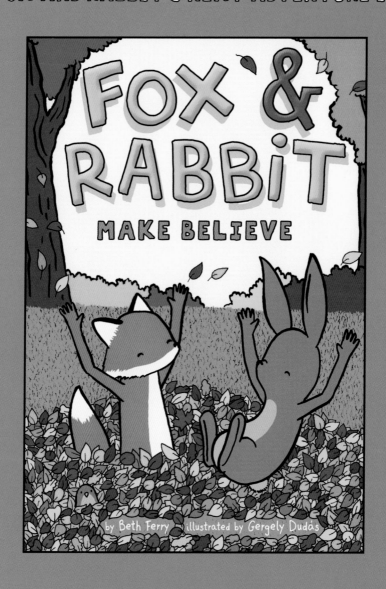

FOX & RABBIT

MAKE BELIEVE

by Beth Ferry   illustrated by Gergely Dudás

MONEY, MARSHMALLOWS & MMMMMM

Hooray! Hooray!
We have all this money.

From what?

From our lemonade stand!
Don't you remember?

Of course I do!
Hooray!

Has anyone seen Tortoise? That slowpoke always misses everything.

I'll get extra to share—just in case.

I'd like a triple scoop of chocolate, peanut butter, and vanilla with a honey drizzle, gummy worms, and 10 marshmallows on top. And fudge sauce.

Cause fudge starts with F.

Do you think Fred wants anything?

Maybe just a marshmallow. Fred doesn't like ice cream.

Yum!

Did you even taste it?

Not really.

Do you see what I see?

I see my very delicious ice cream cone being eaten **very** slowly. What do you see?

ABOUT THE AUTHOR

Beth Ferry is as sure as sand and salt water and sunshine that living by the beach in New Jersey is the perfect place for her. The stories in this book were inspired by the adventures of her three children as they explored their little slice of the world. Sparrow would contend that the best slice in life is a pizza slice, and Beth would have to agree; she completely relates to Sparrow, who is a true adventurer when it comes to food. Beth is the author of many books for young readers, including *Caveboy Crush*, *The Scarecrow*, and the *New York Times* bestselling *Stick and Stone*. Like Fox, she believes in fun and family and friends, which all start with the awesome letter F. You can learn more at bethferry.com.

ABOUT THE ILLUSTRATOR

Gergely Dudás is a self-taught illustrator. The name Dudás means *bagpiper*, but he is not (yet) a self-taught bagpiper, though he does play a few other instruments. Gergely was born in July 1991. His artwork in the early 1990s was a lot more abstract than it is today. He is the creator of the Bear's Book of Hidden Things seek-and-find series.

Like Fox and Rabbit, Gergely loves adventures big and small. And, like Sparrow, he loves all kinds of food (except liver and eggplant). He lives with his girlfriend, a dog, and a dwarf rabbit called Fahéj, which means *cinnamon*. He has more pocket watches than pockets.

Gergely's work is inspired by the magic of the natural world. You can see more from him at dudolf.com.

FOR ANNIE, A WONDERFUL WRITER
AND A SUPER-TROOPER FRIEND
—B.F.

A BOOK ABOUT FRIENDSHIP
FOR MY DEAR FRIEND, BARNI
—G.D.

The art in this book was created with graphite and ink and colored digitally.

Cataloging-in-Publication Data has been applied for and may be obtained from the Library of Congress.

Paperback ISBN 978-1-4197-4695-6

Text copyright © 2020 Beth Ferry
Illustrations copyright © 2020 Gergely Dudás
Book design by Steph Stilwell

Published in paperback in 2021 by Amulet Books, an imprint of ABRAMS.
Originally published in hardcover by Amulet Books in 2020. All rights reserved.

Printed and bound in China
10 9 8 7 6 5 4

Amulet Books are available at special discounts when purchased in quantity for premiums and promotions as well as fundraising or educational use. Special editions can also be created to specification. For details, contact specialsales@abramsbooks.com or the address below.

Amulet Books® is a registered trademark of Harry N. Abrams, Inc.

ABRAMS The Art of Books
195 Broadway, New York, NY 10007
abramsbooks.com